"AN ANCIENT EGYPTIAN PROPHECY AND A
CHALLENGING QUEST TO FREE THE GODS — IF YOU
LIKE AN EPIC ADVENTURE STORY COMBINED WITH
GREAT ILLUSTRATIONS, YOU'LL LOVE THIS."

DR JULIE ANDERSON,
DEPARTMENT OF ANCIENT EGYPT AND SUDAN
THE BRITISH MUSEUM

With thanks to Adrian Bott

First published in the UK in 2013 by Usborne Publishing Ltd.,
Usborne House, 83-85 Saffron Hill, London EC1N 8RT, England.
www.usborne.com

Text copyright © Hothouse Fiction, 2013

Illustrations copyright © Usborne Publishing Ltd., 2013

Cover and inside illustrations by Jerry Paris. Coffin illustration by David
Shephard. Map by Ian McNee.

With thanks to Anne Millard for historical consultancy.

The name Usborne and the devices ♀ ⊕ are Trade Marks of
Usborne Publishing Ltd.

A CIP catalogue record for this book is available from the British Library.

ISBN 9781409562085   JFMA JJASOND/13 02930/1
Printed in Dongguan, Guangdong, China.

INTO THE UNDERWORLD

USBORNE

QUEST of the GODS

DESCENT OF THE
SOUL DESTROYER

DAN HUNTER

USBORNE

The Sacred Coffin Text of Pharaoh Akori

I shall sail rightly in my vessel
I am Lord of Eternity
in the crossing of the sky.

Let my heart speak truth;
Let me not suffer
the torments of the wicked!

For the Great Devourer awaits,
And the forty-two demons
howl around the Hall of Judgement.

Let me hold my head upright in honour,
and be spared the claws and teeth
of the Shrieking Ones.

The Eaters of Bones,
let them not touch me.
The Drinkers of Blood,
let them not come near me.
The Winged Ones with Jaws of Iron,
may they pass me by.

And may I remain safe
in the presence of Osiris forever.

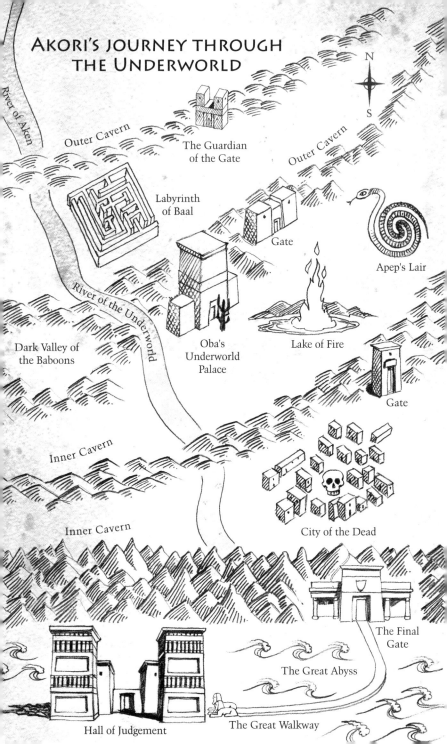

Akori's Journey Through the Underworld

River of Aken

Outer Cavern

The Guardian of the Gate

Outer Cavern

Labyrinth of Baal

Gate

Apep's Lair

River of the Underworld

Dark Valley of the Baboons

Oba's Underworld Palace

Lake of Fire

Gate

Inner Cavern

City of the Dead

Inner Cavern

The Final Gate

The Great Abyss

Hall of Judgement

The Great Walkway

PROLOGUE

The demon-boy, Oba, looked down from the highest tower of his palace in the Underworld. Behind him stood Set, the God of Darkness, whose infernal power had brought Oba back from the brink of death. Oba was dressed in gleaming black armour forged in the deepest pits of his monstrous kingdom. Over his shoulder hung a bow and arrows tipped with cruel, poisoned barbs, like the stings of scorpions. He was ready for war.

Below, his army was gathering. It was so huge it stretched as far as the eye could see, like a nightmarish forest. The soldiers stood clustered so thickly that Oba couldn't see a single scrap of the blood-red earth beneath them.

But they only looked like soldiers from a distance. Up close, their true horror could be clearly seen. For they were dead, every one. Some were grey-fleshed zombies, some were mummies wrapped in yellowed bandages and some were jawless skeletons held together only by the armour they wore. An elite few – sinuous demon slaves, their mouths drooling with hunger – were riding in war chariots drawn by the skeletal remains of horses.

Many of the warriors already bore the marks of deadly wounds, and yet they still stood ready to fight. Their injuries from the living world meant nothing to them now. The soldiers of Egypt would not stand a chance against an enemy who had no fear of death.

"I tell you, we must launch the attack immediately!" Oba insisted. *"We cannot*

wait for Akori to re-enter the Underworld.
I have a plan—"

"Another plan, Oba?" rumbled Set. "And
what would that be? Will you set Baal, Lord
of Thunder against Akori? Or Sokar,
Guardian of Tombs, or the Baboon God,
Babi? Have you forgotten how he defeated
them already?"

Oba frowned. "I mean to send our entire
army against him! We've wasted enough
time. Give the order. We shall march today!"

"Do not presume to order me, boy," Set
growled menacingly. "Have you forgotten
whose power will stand behind your throne
when you are victorious?"

When Oba replied it was with more
respect, although frustration simmered
through every word. "Dark Lord, I beg you.
Our army is ready. Just look at it! We are
strong enough to invade Egypt. Let me attack

Akori's palace and claim it for myself."

Set's eyes glinted red. "And what makes you think Akori will sit meekly on his throne and wait for you to invade his kingdom? He already has four of the Pharaoh Stones. We can be sure he will return to the Underworld to seek the fifth and free my brother Osiris. If we invade too soon and are not here to stop him, he may even succeed. Then our powers over the dead will be destroyed, and we will have no army."

Oba shook his head. "But if we invade Egypt now, I will find him and kill him and he will never set foot in the Underworld again."

Set slammed his huge fist against the wall, causing the whole tower to shudder. "Just like all the other times you planned to kill him?" he roared. "No! We shall remain here in the Underworld. When he arrives in search of the final Pharaoh Stone, we will be ready for him."

"But…my throne—" Oba groaned.

"Be quiet," Set growled. "Do not doubt me. Do as I say and we will defeat that common farm boy once and for all. Then my reign of terror can finally begin."

"So what is your plan, Lord?" Oba snivelled, cowering at Set's outburst.

"I shall lure Akori deep into the Underworld, far from the reach of his allies," Set said, an evil smile spreading across his monstrous snout. "As soon as he is within my grasp, I shall use one of my deadliest servants to exact my revenge. After all, no one can defeat Ammit, the Soul Devourer."

"Ammit?" Oba said, his dark eyes widening. Set nodded.

Oba gasped. "Forgive me for my previous impatience." He bowed before Set. "To see

Akori meet such a terrible end would be well worth waiting for."

Set turned away to the centre of the tower top, where a beacon had been built. With a thunderous roar he breathed twin streams of flame from his nostrils, causing the coals to instantly set alight.

"Servants," roared Set to the troops below. "Today I will destroy Akori. Tomorrow, you will destroy Egypt."

The army of the dead saw the fire go up from the tower. One by one, they raised their arms in salute, and let out a deathly howl.

CHAPTER ONE

Boom-boom. Boom-boom.

Akori rolled over in his bed, clutching his blanket to him. His body wanted to wake up, but his mind kept being sucked down into the blackest of nightmares.

Boom-boom. Boom-boom.

There came the noise again, like a drumbeat. All around Akori, dark energies swirled, sucking him downwards like a whirlpool. He could feel unseen hands grasping at his body and tearing at his tunic.

Boom-boom. Boom-boom.

What *was* that sound? Akori's eyes searched the darkness. But the sound was so loud it seemed to be coming from inside his own body. From the depths of his dream, Akori felt someone's breath, hot and putrid, on the back of his neck.

"Your heart is mine now!" a voice hissed in his ear.

And then, with a sickening jolt, Akori realized where the pounding was coming from. It was his heart – beating louder and faster with fear.

"Noooooow!" the voice howled.

"No!" Akori yelled, sitting bolt upright on his bed.

He looked around the room, taking in the welcome glow of the flickering lamp on the wall. *It was just a dream,* he reassured himself. He was in his bedroom in the palace. Ebe the cat was pacing up and down on the floor beside his bed. Akori felt his heartbeat start to steady.

"Noooooooow!" the howl came again.

Akori sighed. He realized it was coming from outside. It had to be the wind. He was just about to open the shutters to check, when there was a knock on his door.

"Akori, are you awake?" he heard Manu call.

"Yes, come in," Akori replied, getting out of bed.

Manu hurried into the room, clutching a bundle of scrolls. When Ebe saw him she gave a soft purr and coiled around his legs.

"Have you heard the wind?" Manu said. "It sounds as if a terrible storm is on its way."

"I know. It was so loud it gave me nightmares. Did it wake you too?" Akori asked.

Manu shook his head. "I couldn't sleep so I went to the palace library to read some scrolls. But the storm sounds so bad now, I thought I ought to come and warn you."

"You thought well," Akori said, smiling at his friend. "If it gets much louder it will wake the entire palace. I need to be there to reassure my people if there is any damage from the storm. Let's go to the great hall."

As the three friends made their way along the passage to the hall the wind howled again, even louder and more menacing than before.

"I hope there's still a city left by the time the sun comes up," Manu said, nervously. "That wind sounds strong enough to tear the whole place down. Imagine coming out of the palace to see nothing but sand dunes."

"We'll open the palace up to any citizens who've lost their homes," Akori said.

"Anyone is welcome to stay under my roof if they've lost theirs."

When they got to the great hall, the old High Priest was waiting for them with a blanket draped over his shoulders. His aged face was grave. A few servants had gathered at the end of the room, but they weren't waiting on anyone, nor did anyone ask them to. Everyone was retreating to where the walls were thickest, away from the terrible howling of the wind.

"Akori," the old High Priest said, sensing his presence even though he was blind. "I am glad you're here. Unnatural things are happening tonight. We must pray together, and hope the great Gods can hear us over the sound of this fearful windstorm."

Another howl rang out around the palace, as piercing as a vulture's shriek.

Akori shuddered. "It sounds like a

thousand voices, crying out into the night..."
He stopped mid-sentence. Then he grabbed a
burning torch, strode over to one of the many
shuttered windows and flung it open.

Manu ran to his side, alarmed. "What are
you doing?"

"Look!" Akori held the torch outside so that
Manu could see. The flame didn't flicker at
all, and Akori couldn't feel a breath of wind
on his face. None of the buildings he could see
from the window were covered in sand, like
they would normally be in a desert storm. In
fact, they seemed in perfect condition.

"The air's completely still," Manu said,
with a look of dawning horror. "There's no
wind at all."

The endless moaning now rose to a
crescendo, seeming to rush in on them from
everywhere. Akori could even make out
individual voices in the morass of noise –

screams, groans, roars of rage, sobs of grief.

Ebe leaped from the old High Priest's lap onto the table, arched her back and hissed.

The High Priest stood and raised a shaking hand. "Gods be with us all."

"The dead!" Akori gasped. "It must be the dead howling from the Underworld." Shivers rippling along his spine, he swiftly closed the shutters. Dread rose up within him.

"They're closer than ever," the old High Priest said. "Oba and Set must be preparing their attack on your kingdom."

"Then we have to strike first," Manu said, thumping his fist on the table.

Akori looked at his friend. Manu might still be a bookworm at heart, but the quests they had travelled on together had toughened him up, and there was real steel in him now.

"But I only have four of the Pharaoh

Stones," Akori said. "Horus told me I would only be able to defeat them and release Osiris with all five."

"You need to seek counsel from Horus," the old High Priest urged. "Call him from the fire right away. We need his guidance now more than ever." Though the fire was burning brightly, the old man clutched his blanket closely around him, as if to keep out a deadly chill.

Akori rushed to the fire, fell to his knees and stretched his hands out towards the flames. "Horus! Mighty Avenger! Your champion calls upon you. Our enemy is close at hand."

Instantly the flames shot up in a geyser of living light. As the fire blazed with increasing intensity, the image of Horus began to emerge. The God stepped from the fire, his radiant body shimmering with

power and his hawk's head surrounded with a halo like the sun. He stood before Akori, huge and majestic.

"You did well to call upon me, my champion," he said, his voice booming around the hall. "Anubis, Guardian of the Dead, has brought me word of what is happening. The army of the dead is amassing. It won't be long before they strike."

"Do I stay and fight?" Akori asked.

Horus shook his head. "No. There is no time. Your path, once again, leads to the Underworld. You *must* find the final Pharaoh Stone!"

Akori frowned. "But who's going to protect my people from Oba's army if I leave?"

"Akori, your destiny awaits you in the kingdom of the dead – not here," Horus insisted. "I know your heart yearns to stay and defend your beloved Egypt, but Set and Oba can *only* be stopped when all of the Pharaoh Stones have been found."

Akori bowed his head. "I understand."

"The last of the Stones – the Stone of Honour – lies at the very deepest part of the Underworld," Horus went on. "Travel by Aken's barge, for that route is the safest and most direct. He will take you to the final gateway at the heart of the Underworld, and the Hall of Judgement."

Akori's heart sank. Travelling with Aken, the ferryman of the dead, would mean journeying all the way to the Valley of the Kings first, as Akori would need to enter his own coffin. Only then would Aken's barge collect them and take them to the Underworld. It would add hours to their quest, and time was already running out.

"Can't we use the entrance through the

Dark Pharaoh's palace? Wouldn't that be quicker?" Akori asked.

Horus shook his head. "Without Aken, you would have to make your own way to the heart of the Underworld. Who knows what monsters Oba will have awaiting you. No – it will be safer and quicker to travel by Aken's barge." He bent down to look Akori straight in the eye. "When you find the Stone, you will have the power to free my father Osiris. Only then will the dead return to their graves and order be restored to the Underworld. But if you fail, then the dead will overrun the living, and Egypt will be nothing but a mass grave from horizon to horizon."

Akori was just about to thank Horus for his wisdom, when one of his servants began to choke and splutter. Akori turned to see what was wrong. The servant's face was flexing and contorting like a nest of vipers. His eyes bulged and the veins stood out on his bald head. He pointed a finger that quivered like an arrow in a dying man's chest. When he spoke, the voice that burst from his throat was not human. It was deep and bestial. "Osiris will remain imprisoned for ever!" it rasped.

The guards ran to seize the servant.

"Leave him!" Akori ordered.

"Give up the fight now, fools…or suffer for all eternity," gurgled the man.

"He's possessed," Manu said. "It's Set. He's speaking through him as if he were a puppet."

The servant pointed his trembling finger towards the fire. A vision appeared in the flames. It was of Osiris, lying bound in mummy wrappings. His noble face was filled with pain and gashed with wounds. The mighty God struggled, but he was clearly too weak to break free.

The servant lurched towards Horus. "Behold your father," he taunted with Set's voice. "See the fate of the mighty Osiris – the same fate that awaits you."

"Be silent, evil one!" Horus bellowed. "By all the powers of light, I cast you out!"

Horus brandished his *ankh*, a looped cross – the symbol of life. It shone white hot as if it had been drawn from the forge.

Set gave a long, hoarse laugh from the servant's mouth, before the man was suddenly thrown backwards against the wall as if by an invisible force.

The vision faded from the fire. Manu ran to tend to the servant. He was groaning in pain; all the colour drained from his face.

"Set will pay for this," Akori said angrily. "I swear it."

"You have to hurry," Horus urged. "Osiris *must* be freed. Only then will Egypt be safe."

"I won't let you down, My Lord," Akori promised. "Once I have the last Stone, I will free your father. And then I will stop Set and Oba once and for all."

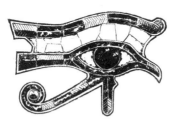

CHAPTER TWO

There was no time for lengthy goodbyes.
Akori, Manu and Ebe set off for the Valley
of the Kings after only the briefest of
blessings from the old High Priest. Akori
looked over his shoulder at his palace as
they left, drawing his cloak around him,
his *khopesh* safe in its hilt. The guards
were all at their stations. He silently
prayed for their safety, with one hand on
his golden armour from Montu, God of
War. Just sensing the four powerful Pharaoh

Stones beneath his fingers calmed Akori.

Eventually, they arrived at the Valley. Akori wished there had been some other way to enter the Underworld. The journey there had taken hours already. How long would it be before Oba's army of the dead attacked Egypt? Horus had assured them that travelling with Aken the ferryman would be the safest and easiest way of reaching the final gateway in the Underworld. Akori knew he must put his faith in the God, but, as he, Manu and Ebe all lay together inside his coffin, he couldn't help feeling anxious.

"No matter how many times we do this, I'll never get used to it," Manu whispered in the darkness.

Blue hieroglyphs began to appear in front of them, scratched on the inside of the coffin lid by an invisible hand.

"Another coffin text," Akori murmured.

The last two times they had journeyed to the Underworld in his coffin, these magical texts had appeared to help them on their quest. Akori hoped this one would provide some clues about where to find the final Pharaoh Stone.

Together, Akori and Manu began to read the glowing words aloud.

I shall sail rightly in my vessel,
I am Lord of Eternity in the crossing of
the sky.
Let my heart speak truth;
Let me not suffer the torments of the
wicked!
For the great Devourer awaits,
And the forty-two demons howl around
the Hall of Judgement.
Let me hold my head upright in honour,
And be spared the claws and teeth of the
Shrieking Ones…

Images of the horrific creatures awaiting them began to dance in Akori's mind like the shadows cast by firelight on a cave wall. A third voice was reading the text with them, as it had before. But this time the voice was rasping and inhuman, just like the voice from his dream. It sounded eager and excited, as if it couldn't wait for Akori to come to the Underworld. Akori shuddered as he wondered who the mysterious voice belonged to.

The coffin started rocking wildly. The glowing hieroglyphs danced crazily in front of them. Ebe mewed in panic and scrabbled about, ripping at the coffin wood with her claws. But the sinister voice continued hissing into Akori's ears.

The Eaters of Bones, let them not touch me.
The Drinkers of Blood, let them not come
 near me.

*The Winged Ones with Jaws of Iron, may
they pass me by…*

The coffin shuddered and went into free fall. Akori knew what this meant. They were passing from the living world into the Underworld on Aken's barge.

The mysterious voice roared the last words of the coffin text: *…And may I remain safe in the presence of Osiris for ever!* Then the script vanished, leaving them alone in complete darkness. For a few seconds there was total silence, then the *splosh, splosh, splosh* of Aken's oars began.

Akori sighed with relief. "Seems like we made it." Gingerly, he lifted the coffin lid and sat up. Aken, the strange backward-headed ferryman, didn't even turn around. He never paid any attention to his passengers.

They were drifting slowly down the black river. Great arches of rock rose over them like sculptures made by giants. Shores of deep-red sand stretched far into the distance.

"I suppose we stay on board until we see the final Gate," he said.

Manu nodded. "The Hall of Judgement is in the very depths of the Underworld. After that, Aken begins his journey back to the living world."

"So, how much do you know about the Hall of Judgement?" Akori asked.

Manu immediately frowned. Ebe hissed and curled herself behind his legs. "Enough to know that I'm not looking forward to going there," Manu said.

Akori looked at him questioningly. "Why?"

Manu huddled closer and lowered his voice to a whisper. "You know how when the dead are mummified their brains and other internal organs are removed from their bodies and stored in jars?"

Akori grimaced at the thought. "Yes."

"Well, one organ is kept inside the body."

Akori nodded. "The heart."

"That's right." Manu moved even closer. "The heart is taken out and weighed when the dead person gets to the Hall of Judgement."

Akori couldn't help shivering.

"Osiris would weigh the heart against the feather of Maat, to see if the person had been good or bad. If the heart was as light as the feather it meant that the person had been good and Osiris would allow them to pass on to the afterlife in the Fields of the Blessed."

Akori looked at Manu. "And if it was heavier?"

"Then the person would be condemned to stay in the Underworld for ever. And their heart…" Manu broke off.

"What?"

"Their heart would be fed to Ammit – the Devourer of Souls."

Akori gulped. All Egyptians lived in fear of having their soul eaten by Ammit. Once, only the sinful and wicked had reason to fear her. But now that Oba ruled the Underworld, who knew whose side she was on?

"Look, there's the first Gate," Manu said, pointing to it in the distance.

Akori thought back to how he'd had to fight the gruesome Guardian of the Gate on his first quest to the Underworld. He'd only managed to defeat the monster by allowing it to swallow him whole and then cutting his way out of its stomach. Back then it had seemed as if nothing could be worse. Yet every time he had journeyed to the Underworld he'd encountered an even deadlier foe. If he had to fight Ammit for the final Stone then Set

37

had been saving the very worst for last.

The three friends sat in silence as Aken steered his barge through the desert region. The firelit towers of Oba's palace appeared on the horizon, glinting red like demons' eyes.

"I wish I could get off right now and bring that fiend Oba to justice," Akori muttered under his breath.

"There isn't time," Manu warned.

"I know." Akori sighed. "It's just that seeing his palace so close…"

"Once you free Osiris, he'll tear that place down in a heartbeat," Manu said.

"*If* I can free Osiris," Akori replied softly. "None of us knows what the future holds, not even the Gods. We're heading into unknown territory now."

They fell back into silence as the barge glided past the sinister palace and into a part of the Underworld they hadn't seen before. Craggy mountains, as black as the night sky, loomed up on either side of them.

"I'm glad we came in the barge now," Manu said. "This looks creepier than any of the places in the Underworld we've visited before."

Ebe purred her agreement.

"Me too," Akori said, looking up at the mountain peaks, where red lightning bolts crackled and sparked.

"Look at the caves," Manu said.

Akori peered into the darkness. The mountainside they were passing was dotted with gaping cave mouths, great stalactites hanging down from their roofs like predators' teeth. All of a sudden a flapping sound echoed throughout the ravine. Akori saw a sudden movement from one of the caves. Something huge was flying out at them, approaching the barge at speed.

Before they had time to take shelter in the coffin, the thing was upon them. It was one of the most hideous creatures Akori had ever seen. It had the face of a crazed woman, surrounded by long, straggly hair. But its body was that of a vulture. Huge greasy wings sprouted from her back. The creature roared into Akori's face, revealing a mouth full of fangs, grey as iron nails. Nearby, another of the beasts emerged from a different cave.

"Demon vultures!" Manu screamed. "They'll eat us alive!"

CHAPTER THREE

The demon vultures circled overhead, the flapping of their huge wings causing the barge to rock wildly. Aken gripped his oars to steady himself and turned his backward-facing head from side to side, trying to see what was causing the commotion.

Akori gripped his *khopesh* and Manu clung on to the coffin. Ebe snarled as she shifted into her wildcat form, growling at the demon vultures menacingly.

A screech, quickly followed by another,

told Akori that the foul creatures were on the attack again. They came in on a power dive, claws outstretched, wings spread. Aken flailed around with one of his oars, swiping at them as they went past.

The two vultures broke formation in mid-air. One of them came hurtling down towards Akori, while the other zoomed over his head. Ebe roared and leaped up, sinking her claws into the vile beast's side.

The demon vulture gave a half-human, half-birdlike shriek, its legs kicking wildly. It tried to stab Ebe in the throat with its huge claws. Akori slashed at its wing with his sword, and it squealed in pain. It struggled out of Ebe's grasp and took to the air, feathers fluttering down in its wake. Its movements were faltering and lopsided. *It won't get far on that injured wing,* Akori thought grimly.

43

A yell came from behind him.

Akori spun around, just in time to see the other vulture snatch Aken up in its claws. Akori leaped forward and thrust, but the blow just missed the retreating creature. It beat its wings and rose out of Akori's reach. Aken struggled in its grip, bellowing.

"Oh no you don't!" Akori yelled. He swung the *khopesh* upwards, slicing at the back of the demon vulture's legs. With a blood-curdling screech it released Aken and took to the sky. The ferryman fell and landed heavily on the deck, setting the whole boat rocking.

Akori watched the two injured beasts disappear into their caves. For now, at least, they had gone.

"Akori!" Manu said urgently. "Aken's hurt."

Akori hurried over to the stricken ferryman, who was lying on his side next to the coffin. There was a huge gash on the top of his arm where the vulture's talons had dug into his flesh.

Aken looked up at Akori. His nostrils flared as he took deep, pained breaths. Akori felt strange. It was as if the God had finally noticed him, after all this time.

"I'm sorry," Akori said. "I thought those things were coming to attack us, but now I think Oba sent them to attack you."

Manu touched Aken's wounded arm, and the mysterious ferryman moaned in pain.

"Don't worry," Akori said. "We'll take care of you."

But, to Akori's surprise, Aken began shaking his backwards head.

"You must complete your quest," the ferryman said. His voice was as deep and soft as the wind through the rushes.

"You know!" Akori exclaimed.

Aken nodded. "Yes, Pharaoh. My master, Ra, has ordered me to ferry you anywhere you need to go in the Underworld. I know all about you and your brave adventures. But you mustn't let me keep you. You have to go."

"But you're injured, I can't—" Akori began.

"If you don't release Osiris a worse fate will befall all of Egypt," Aken interrupted. "You have no time to lose." Ebe mewed her agreement.

"Well, at least let me bind your wound before we go." Akori ripped the bottom off his cloak and tied it tightly around Aken's arm.

"I suppose we can follow the riverbank to the Hall of Judgement," Manu said.

"No," said Aken, who was frowning and shaking his head. "It will take too long," the ferryman explained. "You will have to take the shortcut through the City of the Dead."

"The City of the Dead?" Manu looked puzzled. "What is that?"

"It is a terrible place," Aken said, with a grimace. Akori couldn't tell if it was from pain or fear. "Ever since Osiris has been imprisoned, the dead have been amassing in the Underworld. There are so many now, they have created their own terrible city. You must take great care. Without Osiris in charge, there is no order any more. The bad souls have all gone back to their evil ways – the ways which got them condemned to punishment in the Underworld in the first place. And the others, even the good ones, are filled with rage and frustration, their souls unable to find peace, awaiting a judgement that never comes."

"How do we get to this city?" Akori asked.

"Take the pass, over there," Aken said, pointing to a narrow passageway cutting through the mountainside. "Follow it to the end and you shall come out in the city." He slumped back down onto the deck.

"Hide inside my coffin until we return," Akori said. "It will protect you from any further attack." Slowly he and Manu raised the heavy lid, then they helped Aken clamber in.

The ferryman looked up at Akori and gave him a grateful smile. "Good luck, brave Pharaoh," he murmured, "may the good Gods be with you."

Akori nodded his thanks, before lowering the lid of the coffin.

"We need to hurry," he said, turning to Manu and Ebe. "If those demon vultures return while we're out in the open, we're dead meat. And we need to get to the Hall of Judgement before Oba launches his attack on Egypt."

Ebe had returned to her small form, and Akori scooped her up. Then he and Manu jumped down into the murky water and waded over to the riverbank. The mountain pass gaped in front of them, a seemingly endless black void. It didn't exactly look welcoming but anything was better than having to face another vulture attack. Akori set Ebe down onto the ground. She shook herself vigorously, even though she had only got slightly wet.

"Let's go," Akori said, and the three friends began running into the darkness.

After what felt like for ever, Akori saw a dim red glow at the end of the pass. "I think we're almost there," he panted over his shoulder at the others.

Ebe went racing ahead. A couple of minutes later she returned and gave a low hiss of warning.

"Uh-oh," Manu muttered.

Akori gripped the hilt of his *khopesh*.

They came to a halt at the end of the pass. Down below, in the red-tinged gloom, Akori could see the roofs of many buildings. Fires were burning in open squares and dark silhouettes could be seen coming and going in the streets. *The City of the Dead*, Akori thought with a shudder, just as Aken had said. At the far side it seemed as if the ground itself was moving. Fresh despair closed in as Akori realized that it was actually hundreds of people, all marching in strict formation.

"Oba's army!" Manu gasped.

"Quick," Akori said, already starting to clamber down the mountainside. "They're still at the other side of the city. Hopefully if we hurry we can evade them."

"But there are so many of them," Manu

said, his eyes wide with shock.

Akori nodded. "Exactly. If I don't find the final Stone soon, Oba will unleash them upon Egypt and my people will perish."

Without another word, the trio scrambled their way down the mountainside and made their way to the nearest street. It was swarming with dead souls, some of them transparent and ghostly, some skeletal, and many mummified. Tension hung in the air like a river mist.

"Why do they all look so angry?" Akori whispered, as they edged past a crowd of moaning, decrepit figures.

"It's like Aken said. If they can't pass through judgement to the afterlife, they can never find rest," Manu whispered back.

Akori shuddered as the crumbling bones of a dead soul rattled against his arm in the throng of the crowd. "Let's try and get through here quickly. This place gives me the creeps," Akori muttered.

"This passage looks a bit quieter," Manu said, nodding towards a narrow walkway. "Let's try down here."

But when they got to the end of the passage they saw a sight that almost made Akori's heart stop. A division of Oba's army stood in formation in the square in front of them, going through battle drills. Akori's muscles tensed as he watched the rows of skeletal figures marching back and forth.

"Come on," he whispered and they turned and raced back down another side street. At the end they turned a corner and found themselves in a market. Dead fishermen wearily went through the motions of selling fish, but the fish they held up were rotting on the bone. Dead merchants held up sheets of tattered cloth, boasting about the quality.

They all seemed completely unaware that their goods were falling to pieces.

A skull-faced beggar held up his hand to a passing mummy and whined for help. The mummy smacked it in irritation and the hand flew off, landing in a gutter.

"What do we do now?" Akori whispered in frustration. "Ask someone for directions?"

The air was thick with brimming tension. The dead swarmed about the market stalls, eyeing the decaying food. The stench was overwhelming. Almost suffocated by the heat and the crowds, Akori kept walking, anxious not to look out of place, or meet the gaze of any of the dead.

Traders waved maggoty meat at him. "Fresh today!" they yelled. "Look at the quality!" A sunken-eyed ghoul held out a bowl of dates that were grey with mould.

"This is hopeless," Akori protested. "How

are we ever going to find the Hall of
Judgement?"

Suddenly Manu's face lit up. "Akori! Look!
The mummy over there, the one with the
stall full of scrolls – his sign says he's a map
seller!"

CHAPTER FOUR

Akori, Manu and Ebe walked hesitantly towards the dead map seller's stall. Seeing them approach, the mummy rubbed his bony hands together, sending a shower of dust over the scrolls in front of him.

"Blessings of the endless night be upon you, travellers," he said in a creaky, rattling voice. "Oh, it's good to see some young ones here. One grows so tired of the same old decaying faces."

"We're looking for a map of the

Underworld," Akori said, resting his hand on the hilt of his *khopesh*. Something about the greedy way the mummy was looking at him made him nervous.

The mummy scratched his chin, sending flakes of fetid skin tumbling to the ground. "But of course you are," he grumbled. "Ever since the mighty Set and great Pharaoh Oba seized control of the Underworld, every soul has been doomed to wander lost about this land. Fortunately I can be of some assistance to you." He spread out a sheaf of scrolls in front of them. "Which part of the Underworld do you need a map of?"

"We need to get to the Hall of Judgement," Akori explained.

The mummy took a step back. "The Hall of Judgement?" He shook his withered head. "I would advise you not to venture there. They say the mighty

Set does not welcome visitors."

Akori's heart quickened. Was that where Set was lurking in wait for him? He realized with sudden urgency that if Set was in the Hall of Judgement, perhaps that would be where he would find Osiris too.

Thinking quickly, Akori said, "We wish to honour Lord Set and we need a map directing us to the hall. Do you have one?"

"Oh, I do," the mummy said. "But first there is the small matter of payment."

"We can pay," Akori assured him. "Just give us the map. Please." He looked at Manu anxiously. Time was running out.

The mummy reached down below the stall and fetched up a papyrus scroll. "Here," he said, showing the map to Akori. "But such treasures do not come cheap."

Akori gave the mummy a pouch full of bronze nuggets. "It's all we have," he said.

"It's good quality bronze. You could buy stacks of papyrus for that!"

The merchant tipped the nuggets into his hand and let them rattle through his bony fingers onto the dusty ground. "Useless."

"But it's very valuable!" protested Akori.

"Maybe in the living world," leered the mummy, "but down here such trinkets are worthless. Didn't you learn *anything* when your embalmers prepared your body for burial?"

Akori remembered he was supposed to be playing the part of a dead soul. "Erm… I suppose I forgot a lot of things."

"They weren't very careful when they took his brain out," Manu added helpfully. "I think someone dropped it when they were trying to put it in the jar."

"Maybe you have something else to exchange," the mummy said with a grin.

Something black and leathery poked through his jaws and stroked his yellow teeth. Akori thought it was a scarab at first, then he realized it was the creature's decaying tongue. "Perhaps that fine sword of yours?"

"I don't think so," Akori said firmly. "Come on, Manu. We'll go somewhere else."

"Wait!" said Manu. "What about my cloak?" He took it off and held it out to the merchant. Although it was a very plain material, it was well made and in reasonably good condition.

The merchant coughed, shooting puffs of dust out of the holes in his nose. He reached out a hand and examined the cloak.

"Hmm," he said, turning it over. "Not bad. But not enough to pay for the map."

Akori was ready to turn and leave, but Manu held firm and continued to

barter. "This cloak is made from the finest Egyptian cotton."

"But it is so plain," argued the merchant.

"That will only increase its appeal," countered Manu. "It will be to everybody's taste."

The mummy frowned. "Alright," he sighed. "It is a deal." He took Manu's fleshy palm in his bony hand and they shook on it. Then he handed Manu the map.

"That was brilliant, Manu," Akori whispered in his friend's ear. "Now come on, let's get out of here."

They were almost past the stall when Akori felt the dry, brittle bones of the mummy's hand on his forearm.

"Wait!" he said. "The little cat is yours, yes?"

Ebe curled herself around Akori's feet.

"Yes, what of it?" Akori said, frowning.

"I've changed my mind. I want her instead. Take your cloak back." The mummy was already striding out from behind the stall. He snatched Ebe up in his arms before Akori could react. She let out a startled mew.

"She's not for sale!" Akori snapped. "Give her back!"

"Everything is for sale in this place, boy," snarled the mummy. "Her skin will make an excellent binding."

"But you've already accepted the cloak as payment," said Manu. "We shook on it. A deal's a deal."

The mummy laughed, wheezing out great clouds of dust and sand. "So? With Osiris gone, who's going to judge me now?"

"Give her back!" Akori demanded and, using all his strength, he pulled Ebe out of the mummy's clutches. Ebe scrambled gratefully into his arms, accidentally scratching him with one of her claws.

"Ouch!" Akori muttered. A thin line of blood appeared across his forearm.

The mummy stopped and stared. "Blood!" he hissed, his tongue flicking hungrily between his teeth. "You're not dead!" he shouted. "You're *alive*!"

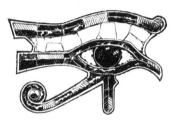

CHAPTER FIVE

"Run!" Akori yelled, turning on his heel, ready to flee from the market.

"He's alive! He's alive!" the map seller continued to screech. A crowd of the dead started gathering around the stall, moaning and hissing.

"Just one question, Akori," Manu said. "Where do we run *to*?"

"This way!" Akori shouted, barging through the crowds of dead souls towards a small alleyway.

"Stop them!" the map seller cried. "They do not belong here. They are not dead!"

"Call for the army!" another voice shouted. "They'll soon catch them."

"Call for the army!" The cry started spreading through the market like wildfire. Akori's heart sank as he heard it rippling out into the surrounding streets. How long before it reached the soldiers who had been practising their drills just a block away? How long before the vast ranks of soldiers he'd seen from the mountain pass heard the call?

"Follow me!" Akori yelled to Manu and Ebe.

They fled down the alley and came out into a narrow side street, bustling with yet more dead people. Akori glanced over his shoulder and saw a sight that made his blood freeze. A rank of Oba's soldiers were pounding their way down the alleyway after them, swords aloft.

"Akori, they've blocked off the road!" Manu cried.

Akori looked ahead to the end of the street. A small group of guards had moved to barricade the exit. They stood glaring, brandishing their spears.

"Summon mighty Set!" one of them shouted. "He must hear of this!"

"That's the last thing we need," Akori gasped. "We have to get out of here, and fast."

But how? he thought to himself. *There's no way out.* He heard a loud hiss behind him and turned to see Ebe changing into her Goddess form. The dead around them began to gasp. Ebe flicked her head at Akori and Manu, gesturing to her back.

"She wants us to get on," Akori yelled.

"But is she strong enough to carry both of

us out of the city?" Manu cried.

"We just have to hope so. Come on!"
Akori leaped onto Ebe's back, with Manu
right behind him. The rank of sword-waving
soldiers was almost at the end of the
alleyway.

"I hope this works," Akori said. "Hold on,
Manu!"

With a tremendous bound, Ebe launched
herself over the startled crowd and landed on
the flat roof of the nearest building. Akori
heard the soldiers below yelling in
frustration. But Ebe ran faster than a loosed
arrow, bounding from one rooftop to the
next.

Every time Ebe landed after a jump Akori
felt the air being jolted from his lungs. He
held on tight, digging his fingers deep into
the fur of her neck.

"We've lost them!" Manu said joyfully,

looking down into the street below. "They'll never catch us now!"

"Get us away from the city, Ebe," Akori called. "Over there looks good, where the road runs up into that rocky gorge. We'll find somewhere to hide and check the map."

Ebe ran on and on, breathing in great gasps. Akori could tell she was getting tired.

"Thanks, Ebe," Akori said fondly. "You saved our lives."

But Ebe made no reply. She ran and ran, panting, as she sped across the blood-red sand that spread out beyond the city. Eventually, they reached the dusty road that led up into the rocky ground beyond. To Akori's relief the place was completely deserted.

They clambered off Ebe's back. She immediately rolled onto her side and shrank back to her small cat form. Akori stroked her, doing his best to comfort her.

"Ebe, are you alright?" asked Manu.

Ebe gave a small mew, sat up and began to clean herself. She glanced up at Akori as if to say, "Don't worry, I'm okay." Akori sighed with relief, then looked at Manu, who was already unrolling the map.

"We need to find the quickest route to the Hall of Judgement," Akori said. "We've lost so much time. Oba's army could strike at any moment."

"I know," said Manu as he stared at the map. He was silent for a moment, then he turned to Akori and smiled. "That map seller may not have been very nice, but he really knew his maps. This is a masterpiece! Just look at the detail."

Akori frowned. "I don't want to frame it and hang it on the palace wall, Manu. I just want you to read it. Where *are* we?"

"Not far from the last Gate." Manu pointed to the image of a huge doorway, set into the side of a rock face. "It leads to the deepest region of the Underworld, the part the map calls the Great Abyss."

"So that's where the Hall of Judgement is?"

Manu nodded. "And then beyond that lie the Fields of the Blessed – where the souls of the good are finally rewarded. I'm hoping things start getting a lot better the closer we get to it."

Akori tried to hold onto that thought as they began making their way through the rocky terrain, nervously watching for any sign of an attack. The high cliffs and huge boulders could easily hide any number of ambushers. But nothing leaped out at them, nor did anything swoop screaming down from the sky. When he finally caught sight of the majestic gateway carved out of the cliff-face up ahead his spirits lifted even further – only to come crashing down when he saw what was standing in front. Terror rippled through him as he took in the creature guarding the Gate.

The figure was like a man with a lion's head. But unlike the Goddess Sekhmet, who was also lion-headed, there was nothing noble in *his* appearance. Foul, crusted blood stained his mane and his bared fangs. From his waist hung a belt where white, picked-clean bones dangled, rattling as he moved.

The creature sniffed at the air. "I smell flesh," he hissed. "And blood. Living blood! Come closer, little manikins. Let Shezmu taste you."

"Shezmu?" Akori said, fearfully turning to Manu for an answer.

"The Slaughterer of Souls!" Manu replied,

73

rooted to the spot with fear. "He's not a God, Akori. He's a demon. Even the dead fear him. They say…they say he crushes his enemies' heads in a wine press – and drinks their blood!"

"All true," Shezmu said, and a long tongue emerged from his mouth to lick his blood-caked jaws. "Blood is my wine, yes, yes. And bones, so good to chew."

Akori gripped his *khopesh*. "Stand aside, Shezmu, whatever you are! We're going through that Gate!"

Shezmu laughed. "Three against one? That's not very honourable, little warrior."

"Don't listen to him!" Manu begged. "He's stronger than any of us."

"I challenge you," Shezmu said, pointing at Akori. "Single combat. You and me."

Akori looked at him questioningly. "A duel?"

Shezmu nodded. "If you win, you may pass. If you lose, you become fresh fruit for my wine press!"

Akori's mind raced. He was Pharaoh, and being Pharaoh meant having honour at all times. Even if Shezmu was a demon, he'd challenged Akori to a duel. Akori could not refuse. And besides, he couldn't put Manu and Ebe in danger. If Shezmu wanted to fight Akori alone, at least his friends would not be at risk.

"I have to fight him, Manu," he said. He lowered his voice. "Even if I *am* facing him alone, I have got four of the Pharaoh Stones. That's a big advantage."

"That's true," Manu said. "And you won them fair and square." The young priest eyed the demon suspiciously. "I still don't trust him, though."

"I don't either," agreed Akori. "But I can't

back down. And he's blocking our entrance to the Gate. We don't have a choice if we want to get to the Hall of Judgement."

"Just be careful," Manu warned.

But Akori was already walking forward, pointing his *khopesh* at Shezmu.

"Demon, Slaughterer of Souls," he said. "I accept your challenge."

CHAPTER SIX

Akori got into a fighting stance in front of Shezmu, the monstrous demon.

"Put your fancy sword away," Shezmu snarled. "We fight with these." He threw a crude bronze dagger at Akori's feet.

"Very well," Akori said, passing his *khopesh* to Manu to hold. "If it's a fair fight you want, that's what you'll get."

Shezmu grinned horribly and brandished his dagger. It looked razor-sharp.

Akori glanced at his own blade. The edge

was dull and the point was blunt. So, that was Shezmu's idea of honourable fighting, was it? Suddenly, using the Pharaoh Stones didn't seem like an unfair advantage at all.

"Come on!" Shezmu roared and, with that, he launched a blindingly fast attack.

Akori barely had time to call upon the Stone of Speed to match him. Shezmu's blade sliced the air around him with frantic speed, making cuts and slashes that would have ripped Akori to ribbons if he hadn't dodged in time. Even with the Stone of Speed empowering Akori, Shezmu was still almost too fast for him.

Akori ducked a stabbing blow that came right at his eye. So far he hadn't even had the chance to get in a single blow of his own – not that his blunt bronze dagger would have done any good. He circled around and dodged yet another sweeping slash.

"Stand still!" Shezmu raged.

Akori called on the Stone of Strength and elbowed Shezmu hard in the guts. The bones on Shezmu's belt rattled as he flew back through the air, landing hard on his rump. He grimaced, flipped backwards to land on his feet again, and came running in to attack.

This time, Akori dodged the dagger, only for Shezmu to follow up with a swipe from his claws and a bite. The claws raked across Akori's armour, making a sound like a pitchfork dragged across a chest full of coins.

"I thought we were fighting with daggers!" Akori yelled.

"Stop your whining," Shezmu growled. "I'll fight you with whatever weapons I like! You'll be dead soon anyway, so what does it matter?"

Akori knew then that Shezmu was

prepared to do anything to kill him. Well, he might not have any honour, but Akori did. And Akori had other things on his side, too.

Intelligence, for one! Keeping his distance from the dagger and the claws, Akori touched the Stone of Intelligence. *I have to find some weakness in Shezmu's fighting style,* he thought urgently. *Some way I can win this without cheating.*

Instantly he saw what Shezmu was doing. The demon was focusing his attention on Akori's unarmoured neck. No matter whether he attacked with claws, mouth or dagger, he never took his eyes off that spot. Akori recalled Shezmu's words. *"Blood! Living blood! Come closer…let Shezmu taste you."*

Akori leaped backwards out of Shezmu's reach. Then he deliberately lowered his guard, bringing his weapon hand behind his back as if he were preparing for a mighty blow. His neck was completely unprotected now. Shezmu could bite through it in an instant. Akori would be dead and the demon could drink his fill.

Shezmu licked his lips. He bared his teeth and sprang, launching himself at Akori's exposed neck.

Akori called upon the Stone of Strength, grappled Shezmu mid-leap and pulled him to the ground. As the startled demon struggled, Akori wrenched his arm up behind his back. Shezmu roared in pain, letting the dagger fall. Akori snatched up the weapon with his free hand. But there was no need for him to use it. His strength from the Pharaoh Stone was enough to overcome Shezmu.

"I win," Akori grunted. "Yield."

"No!" Shezmu roared. "Never!"

Akori twisted Shezmu's arm harder. The demon howled, as if pain were something completely new to him. "Yield!" Akori repeated, more forcefully this time.

"If I yield, you'll kill me!" Shezmu whined into the dust.

"No, I won't. If you get out of here so we can pass through the Gate, then I promise to let you go."

"Lies! Filthy lies! Why should I believe you?"

"I give you my word of honour," Akori promised.

"Your word as Pharaoh?"

"Yes."

He felt Shezmu go limp in his arms. "I… yield," the demon gasped.

Akori stood up, letting Shezmu go.

Shezmu got to his feet. He scowled, then bowed to Akori in grudging respect. He crossed his arms across his chest and flames suddenly surged up around him, covering him completely. The next moment, the demon was gone. A blackened spot on the sand and a foul stench in the air were all that he left behind.

"You kept your word," Manu said, sounding impressed.

Akori shrugged. "I had to. A promise is a promise, even if you make it to a demon."

Akori and Manu exchanged glances as they stared up at the final Gate. Even their Goddess companion, Ebe, seemed awestruck, winding her way hesitantly between their legs. At last they had reached the heart of the Underworld. Taking a deep breath, Akori and Manu pushed against the Gate with all their might. Gradually it opened to reveal a scene stranger than their wildest imagining.

Instead of the dull rocky landscape on their side of the Gate, there was a broad walkway made from worked stone, with ornamental sphinxes at intervals on either side, stretching far into the distance. Through the mist, Akori could only just make out a white building at the very end. On either side of the walkway was a sheer drop, down to a churning ocean of midnight-black water. To Akori's shock, he realized that nothing appeared to be holding the bridge up. It simply sat, suspended over the ocean, kept in place by the magic of the Underworld.

"The Great Abyss," Manu said in awe. "And that building in the distance must be the Hall of Judgement. We're here, Akori. We've made it!"

"Not yet we haven't," Akori reminded him. "We have to get over this walkway, and there are bound to be guards. We can't risk being seen."

Manu gulped. "Then we'll have to walk along the edge of the walkway and hide behind the sphinxes."

And so the nightmare journey began. All they could do was run, wait and run again, trying not to look down into the giddying drop beneath them. But it was impossible not to. The horror of it seemed to draw their gaze in, like a hideous creature that cannot be looked away from no matter how hard you try. Even sleek, graceful Ebe seemed to tremble as she scampered along the bridge ahead of them.

The mist that weaved its way up from the crashing waves of the Great Abyss was both a blessing and a curse. Its shadowy vapours shrouded the three friends as they made their way across the walkway, so they were all but invisible. But it also swallowed up their feet, making it difficult to see exactly where they placed each step. And simply standing on the walkway was terrifying. Akori could not understand how it felt so solid beneath his feet, when nothing was holding it up. The magic of the Underworld must be more powerful than he could ever have imagined. And yet, he could not keep the terrible fear from his mind that the magic would suddenly fail and send the whole bridge plunging down into the Abyss.

They had got about halfway along the walkway when Akori heard a sinister creaking sound. The trio darted behind the nearest statue, making sure they were completely hidden, and held their breath. The creaking got louder and louder. Akori peered out and what he saw almost made him gasp in horror. A group of strange figures were making their way past them on the bridge. They wore golden funeral masks and long headdresses, and floor-length black cloaks concealed their bodies. As the group went past, one of the cloaks swung open and Akori caught a glimpse of a shrivelled, bony form.

"What are those things?" Akori asked Manu after the strange figures had passed on towards the hall.

Manu frowned. "Osiris's Hall of Judgement is meant to have forty-two wise judges, the Assessors of the Dead, but they don't look anything like *that*. My guess is they're dead souls of some kind. Special ones."

After what felt like hours, they had reached the very last sphinx. The entrance to the Hall of Judgement lay only a short sprint away. The entrance was open, but two vast crocodile-headed beasts guarded it, holding

giant spears. They were easily ten royal cubits tall. They uncrossed their spears as a masked, cloaked figure approached, letting him in.

Inside, Akori could just make out Osiris's throne, surrounded by a gathering crowd of the masked figures. They were all sitting down on benches on either side of the hall, leaving a space in the middle.

"I think I know what's going on," Manu whispered. "Do you remember from the coffin text? *The forty-two demons howl around the Hall of Judgement.* I think those masked mummies have replaced Osiris's forty-two judges of the dead!"

"So where's Oba?" Akori whispered, gripping his sword hilt in anticipation.

Manu shrugged. "Maybe he'll arrive after all the mummies."

Akori sighed. "We're so close. How are we

going to get past those sentries?"

"Fight our way in?" Manu said lamely.

"Not a hope. Those guardians are enormous! I'm good, but I'm not Montu, God of War, even if I have got his armour on!"

"We need a plan," said Manu. "We have to get in there somehow. Once we're in, then we can surprise them. They won't be expecting us to have made it this far."

"Sssh!" interrupted Akori, seeing a figure approach through the mist. They ducked back behind the statue. Akori watched as a cloaked mummy shuffled past them and into the Hall of Judgement. In an instant, a plan came together in his mind, as easily as if he'd read it on a scroll.

"There are forty-two judges in all," he said. "How many are in the hall already?"

Manu quickly counted them. "Thirty-seven."

Akori's eyes lit up. "So there's only a few more left to come! Get ready, Manu. I've got an idea."

They hid and waited until two masked mummies came striding down the walkway. The creatures didn't spare a glance for any of the stone sphinxes that flanked their route as they approached the Hall. So, when Manu and Akori silently slipped out of their hiding place, they didn't even turn around.

There were two soft thumps, followed by the sound of two mummies collapsing, unconscious, to the floor. Akori and Manu quickly dragged them out of sight behind the sphinx. They took the masks, headdresses and cloaks off the stunned mummies and put them on. Ebe darted inside Akori's floor-length cloak, hiding beside his ankles.

"How do I look?" Akori said, trying to keep his tone light. But he was so nervous his heart was threatening to burst out of his chest.

"Terrifying," said Manu. "Gods, I hope this works!" He glanced down at the maskless mummies. "What do we do with them?"

Akori kneeled down and peered into their rotting faces. "They should be out of action for a while. Let's just hope Oba arrives soon. Come on, let's get inside."

They made their way up to the entrance. Through the eyeholes of the golden mask, Akori nervously watched the sentries loom up in front of him. As they turned their heads to look at him, he held his breath and kept walking, forcing himself not to run, not to panic.

Then, very slowly, the sentries uncrossed their spears. Akori drew a deep breath, and then he, Manu and Ebe entered the Hall of Judgement.

CHAPTER SEVEN

We're here at last, Akori thought. *The very heart of the Underworld. In just a few moments, Oba will be here. Then the battle to save my kingdom can finally begin!*

Inside the Hall of Judgement, the masked mummies were seated on benches arranged along the sides of the room. Barbarous symbols had been scrawled on the walls, like graffiti, lit by a few, flickering torches. It hurt Akori's eyes to look at them. At the far end, a throne stood on a dais.

Manu and Akori walked to the back of the hall, careful not to attract any attention. Beneath his cloak, Akori could feel Ebe slinking along beside him, keeping out of sight. No sooner had they taken their seats, when a masked mummy sat down on the other side of Akori. Carefully, Akori pulled his cloak even closer around him, so the mummy wouldn't notice how healthy his flesh looked. The mummy's own flesh was mostly gone, with bones showing through the parchment-thin skin. Beside him, Akori could feel Manu trembling.

A sudden silence fell upon the room. Oba had entered. Akori's heart beat faster at the sight of his old enemy. Beneath the folds of his cloak he clenched his fists, adrenalin coursing through his veins. All of the masked mummies stood, and Akori and Manu hurriedly got to their feet, too. Oba strode over to Osiris's throne and sat down. He waved for the mummies to sit.

"Commanders of my army," Oba declared, spreading his arms wide. "Loyal subjects. The hour of our victory is at hand."

The mummies began to clap. They sounded like sticks rattling together. Akori was glad to see that none of them were carrying weapons. Obviously, being commanders, they were too high and mighty to do any actual fighting. That might work in their favour, he thought.

"The time for our invasion of Egypt is fast approaching," Oba continued. "Mighty Set will remain below to guard the prisoner, Osiris. There have been sightings of that lowly farm boy and his pathetic priest in the City of the Dead. It is only a matter of time before they are crushed once and for all. Meanwhile we will prepare to conquer the upper world. I have assigned each of you a task, which you and your troops must not fail to accomplish." Oba scowled around the hall. "The penalty for failing me is to be devoured by Ammit!"

A gasp of horror rippled around the mummies. Akori glanced at Manu and shuddered.

Oba stood up and began to walk down the central space between the two groups of mummies. "You, General Ankh-af-na-Sutekh, are to burn all the crops south of Thebes. General Thuthmose, you are to despoil the temples of all the Gods who oppose me. I want not one single statue left standing, do you hear?"

The mummy gave a creaky nod.

Oba crossed over to Akori's side of the chamber. "As for you, General Kheti, you will have the honour of leading my personal guard. We will assault Akori's palace and tear each room apart until we find every traitor who has remained loyal to that peasant!"

Oba came even closer, within an arm's length of Akori. "And as for you, General—"

"Now, Ebe!" Akori yelled.

Ebe burst out from beneath Akori's cloak and shifted into her full fighting form. She lashed out on all sides, sending the generals into a screaming panic.

"Protect me, you fools!" shrieked Oba as they started running in every direction.

Akori and Manu tore off their disguises, and Akori unsheathed his *khopesh*. "This is a place of justice, Oba," he shouted. "Now it's time for you to pay for what you've done!"

"Akori?" Oba's voice hissed with pure hatred. "Fool, you challenge me here, at the very seat of my power? Generals, *kill him*!"

The masked mummies began to close in

on Akori, but he was ready. Calling on the Stone of Speed, he span on the spot like a cyclone. The *khopesh* became a blinding circle, shedding golden light into the hall.

As the mummies lunged at him, they were sliced into pieces. Fragments went flying, showering Oba with rotting bits of cloth.

Nearby, Ebe was smashing through the ranks of generals like an unstoppable force. She fought with fearsome efficiency, clawing the mummies down as if they were granary rats.

A few of the mummies had closed ranks to protect Oba, but he obviously didn't have much confidence in them. He was backing away across the hall, screaming orders as he went: "Fools! Idiots! He's only a boy! Can't you *do* something?"

"You should have picked better commanders, Oba!" Akori yelled. He split one mummy down the middle and kicked another into his comrade's arms, knocking them both to the floor.

"I will not be defeated," Oba shouted. "Not again."

Akori advanced on him. "Your time is up, Oba. Give me the Pharaoh Stone."

"I do not have it," Oba replied smugly. "But I know who does. Would you like to meet her?"

Akori looked at him blankly.

Oba threw back his head and gave a blood-curdling cackle. "Ammit!" he screamed at the top of his voice. "Devourer of Souls! Come to me! *Now!*"

There was a sound like distant thunder. The mummies stopped fighting. Ebe and Manu drew away, slinking to the back of the hall like fearful children.

The thundering noise grew louder, until it

sounded like one hundred galloping feet.
The floor shook and the flames of the torches
trembled. Even Oba looked terrified by the
prospect of what he had summoned.

"Oh no," Manu said hollowly. "Not her.
Akori, we have to run."

But it was much too late for that.

Into the room stampeded a living
nightmare.

Ammit towered over Akori in all her
hideous glory. She had the body of a gigantic
hippopotamus, strong, unrelenting and three
times the size of any mortal specimen. Her
forepaws were those of a lioness, her
enormous claws like a row of *khopeshs*,
ready to strike. But her crocodile head was
perhaps the most monstrous feature of all.
Her green scales were as thick as armour,
while her deadly jaws gleamed with razor-
sharp teeth. She wore a headdress of bright

golden armour that glinted menacingly in the light. As she stopped in front of Akori, a putrid stench flooded the entire hall. She smelled like a corpse that had hauled itself up from a marsh – like the stink of death itself.

Akori shivered. He had seen many carvings of evil men being swallowed whole by those grinning jaws. He touched the Stone of Courage, to steady his nerves. Instantly, his trembling stopped.

Manu was not so lucky. As he staggered backwards, overcome by fear, he tripped and fell sprawling across the flagstones. His shaven head struck the floor with a sickening crack.

"Manu!" Akori ran towards him, but Ammit lunged with her jaws and caught Manu up by the leg. She dangled him from her huge teeth and looked at Oba like a dog

waiting to be told it could snap up a treat.

Oba got back into his throne, threw one leg over the arm and gave Akori a gloating leer. "Back when Osiris was in charge of this place," he said, "he used to give the dead a fair trial."

"I know," Akori replied coldly. "And if Set hadn't saved your wretched life, you'd be in Ammit's belly right now!"

"I don't go in for 'fair trials' and all that nonsense," Oba continued.

"That's because you're insane."

Oba frowned at Akori. "Shut up." Then he turned his scornful gaze upon Manu. "I, Pharaoh Oba, Lord of the Underworld, hereby find Manu, Priest of Horus, guilty of being an unbearable know-it-all and pathetic bookworm, who also has the bad taste to count himself a friend of the farm boy, Akori. There is only one punishment for such wickedness! Ammit? Devour him."

"Stop!" Akori yelled.

Ammit looked questioningly at Oba, still holding Manu's limp body in her jaws.

"Judge me in his place!" Akori quickly shouted.

"Oh, *such* honour," Oba grinned. "Such loyalty. He offers himself up, in place of his friend!"

"Do you accept?" Akori demanded.

"Naturally! Congratulations, idiot. You've finally had a good idea for once in your life." Oba rested his chin on his fist. "I shall now pronounce sentence. Akori, farm boy, upstart, pretender to my throne: I hereby find you guilty of sins too numerous to catalogue, and sentence you to be eaten alive on the spot!" He leaned forward to watch, his eyes shining with evil joy. "Take him, Ammit!"

Akori prepared to defend himself. Ebe moved to stand by his side, panting, exhausted but still ready to fight alongside him.

Ammit dropped Manu, turned to Akori and opened her immense jaws wide.

Something caught the light and glittered for an instant among the jagged fangs at the back of her mouth.

Akori's eyes widened. It was a purple stone.

The last of the Pharaoh Stones!

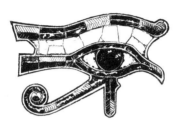

CHAPTER EIGHT

With her mouth gaping open like a cave, Ammit charged.

Akori knew she was going to snap him up as easily as a fly. He couldn't jump down her throat and cut his way out from within, the way he had with the Guardian of the Gate. Those teeth would crunch him up and kill him in an instant, devouring both his body and soul.

Akori dived out of Ammit's way and ran, panting hard, to the other side of the hall.

Ammit came stumbling to a stop, roared, and turned back. Ebe slashed at her leathery flank, but though her claws cut deep, Ammit didn't even seem to notice.

Ammit charged again, snapping her jaws with a sound like a lightning clap. Akori barely got out of the way in time. If he'd been a split second later, his sword arm would have been bitten off at the shoulder. *That would end this fight pretty fast,* he thought grimly.

"That's it! Keep running, you little coward!" Oba crowed from his throne. "Oh, I do hope this lasts for a while. It would be such a pity if it was over too soon!"

As Ammit scrambled back to face Akori, he thrust his *khopesh* into her side. The blade bounced straight off. Ammit grunted in annoyance, as if some small insignificant insect had stung her.

Ebe bounded forwards again and launched herself at Ammit's hideous face, clawing at her eyes. Ammit bellowed and tossed her head from side to side, eventually flinging Ebe off and sending her tumbling across the floor.

Akori ran across the room to the pillars at the far side and braced himself for Ammit's next charge. He racked his brains for some clue, *any* clue, as to how he could win this fight. Ammit kept snapping at Ebe while she skittered back and forth.

Ebe's buying me time, Akori realized. *I have to use that time to plan my next move!*

As he watched Ammit's frustration as she lumbered after elegant Ebe, his mind began to race with new thoughts. Ammit was big, he realized, and powerful, but she wasn't *agile*. Once she began to charge, she couldn't easily stop.

"Don't waste time with the stupid cat-thing!" Oba shouted at Ammit. "It's Akori you're meant to be devouring, not her! Get on with it!"

Ammit turned and roared at Oba, clearly angry. Oba shrank back in his throne, looking fearful, then recovered himself. Akori understood then that Ammit wasn't serving Oba out of choice. Something was forcing her to obey. Could it be the magic of Set?

He struggled to think how he could possibly win against a beast like Ammit. She was the most fearsome of all the creatures in the Underworld. If his *khopesh* didn't even scratch her, how could he beat her? How do you kill the unkillable?

Then, in a flash, he realized, *I don't have to kill her. I just need to get the Stone!*

Ebe yowled as Ammit raked her with her forepaws.

"Get back, Ebe," Akori yelled. "Leave her to me!"

Ammit turned and looked at him curiously. Then, for the first time, she spoke; and her hissing, echoing voice was horribly familiar.

"You would refuse your friend's aid, even though it may mean your death?"

It was the same voice that had spoken to him in his dream and had whispered the Coffin Text with him as they had crossed over into the Underworld. Akori shuddered with horror as he realized Ammit, the monster at the heart of the Underworld, had been aware of his quest all along. She had been watching him, following his progress; judging him perhaps.

Akori swallowed. "Yes."

"But why?"

"Oba is right. It's me you were ordered to devour, not her."

Ammit cocked her head. *"You are a young man of great honour. It is a shame I must kill you. But I am commanded, and I must obey."*

"Very well," Akori said bravely. "Let's get this over with."

Ammit pawed the ground like a bull, and charged.

Akori stood his ground as ten tons of horror came thundering towards him. The pillar's marble surface was cool against his back. His fingers brushed the Stones of Speed and Strength.

At the very last moment, he dodged out of the way.

Ammit couldn't stop. Her prey had suddenly vanished, and she was charging full tilt. She smashed violently into the colossal pillar. An avalanche of stone came tumbling down upon her. Gigantic white chunks slammed into her body and head. She bellowed in agony.

Behind her, Akori had landed on both feet, astounded that he was still alive.

Quickly, he ran to Ammit's head, pinned under fallen masonry. As she opened her mouth to roar again, he thrust his hand inside and closed his hand upon the purple Stone. One powerful tug tore it free.

Ammit made a sound like a long sigh of relief. Foul, warm marshy wind from her lungs ruffled Akori's hair. *"At last. Set's spell is broken. I am free."*

Hardly able to believe it was finally within his grasp, Akori pushed his cloak aside and pressed the last Pharaoh Stone into place on his armour. A blaze of light streamed out from him so bright and powerful it could

only be a thing of legend, a miracle. It blasted the mummies to dust and turned the evil sigils on the wall to crackling ash.

Oba covered his eyes, screaming in agony: "It can't beeeeeee!"

Ammit threw off the fallen masonry that had buried her, shook herself, and stood upright. In the light of the Pharaoh Stones, she looked more majestic than monstrous.

"Pharaoh." She smiled. *"The prophecy is fulfilled."*

"What do you mean?" Akori was confused.

"It was foretold that one day, a Pharaoh would rise who was worthy to bear the five Stones. That day is come. That Pharaoh is you." She bowed her head. *"You have released me from my service to Set and Oba. For that, I will be for ever in your debt. I am yours to command."*

Oba stared in absolute and sheer horror.

"Oh, no. Oh, no, no, no, no."

He got down from the throne.

And he began to run.

CHAPTER NINE

"Not this time, Oba," Akori said. "Ebe, stop him!"

Ebe sprinted after the fleeing demon-boy, pounced and dragged him down to the floor.

"No!" Oba screamed, struggling to pull himself out of Ebe's grasp. "You have no right!" His face lit up with hope. "The Underworld has rules, rules you *must* obey."

"What do you mean?" Akori frowned.

"This hall is for judging the dead. I'm not dead, I'm alive! So you can't judge me.

Ha ha ha!"

"Akori is alive, too, Oba," Ammit said. *"And yet, you judged him. As you said, the Underworld has rules – and you BROKE those rules!"*

Oba's face crumpled again as he realized his hope was false. "Mercy," he begged. "You'll let me go. I know you will."

"It is not up to me," said Akori solemnly. "I do not make the decisions in the Underworld. In Osiris's absence, it is up to Ammit to weigh your soul."

Ammit lifted the struggling Oba by one ankle. He didn't stop screaming. Ebe shrank back to her tiny cat form and lay on the ground, exhausted.

Manu, by now almost fully recovered, sat up and frowned. "You're giving him a chance?" he asked Akori. "Why not just tell her to devour him?"

"Everyone deserves justice," replied Akori. "Even Oba."

"This soul," Ammit said at length, *"is heavy. Evil deeds weigh it down like iron chains. I have never known a soul as laden with sin as this."*

"No," blubbered Oba as he flailed about upside down. "Please…"

Ammit tossed him into the air. As he fell, she opened her jaws wide and devoured Oba whole.

Akori felt a little sickened, but it was the justice of the Gods. Oba was finally gone. Never again would his evil stain the earth.

"Now you must hurry, Pharaoh," said Ammit. *"Past the doors ahead lies a staircase, running deep below the Hall of Judgement. At the very bottom is the cell where Osiris is imprisoned. His life force is almost spent."*

"But Osiris is a God!" Akori said. "Surely his life force is never-ending."

Ammit shook her huge head sorrowfully. *"Set fears he is about to lose. He cannot risk you freeing Osiris. And so, though it has drained his own power greatly, he has begun a final terrible spell. Osiris is being destroyed."*

Manu turned pale. "If Osiris is destroyed, Set will rule for ever. We have to stop him."

"But if Set has drained his power casting this spell, he'll be weakened!" Akori clenched his fists. "Manu, I've got a plan. It might be the craziest thing I've ever thought of, but we've got to try it."

Akori explained his plan, but instead of looking pleased, the young priest was horrified. Ebe mewed plaintively.

"I hate it, Akori," protested Manu. "After everything you've been through; all the battles, all the quests…how could you even think of doing this?"

"Because we have no other choice," Akori said simply.

"But you'll die!"

Akori shrugged. "At least I know I've got a well-made coffin to look forward to. I've seen it enough times."

"Always joking." Manu gave Akori a sad smile, before pulling him into a brisk hug. "Let's get on with it, then. If we're going to do this, let's do it fast."

Once everything was in place, the three friends descended the staircase together. It stretched down into tar-smelling darkness. The few torches that lit their way gave off a stinking black smoke, so it was like groping their way through fog. Akori smelled the foul odour of wild pigs, and knew Set was near. He'd smelled that stench before, when Set had almost destroyed him.

At the bottom was a vast, vaulted chamber. Dozens of thick iron chains hung down from the wooden beams in the ceiling.

Osiris lay on the floor, bound in mummy wrappings, in the centre of a circle scrawled in a sinister red substance. Hieroglyphic designs surrounded him and a ring of lamps bathed him in sickly light. His face looked shrunken, as if it were collapsing from within like a melting wax figurine.

Manu ran into the room and kneeled by Osiris's side. "He's barely alive!"

Akori was shocked and terrified to see Osiris so broken. But he knew he must not panic, and instead, put his faith in Manu to do as they had agreed. Akori had to put all his energies into fighting Set.

"I know you're here, Evil One!" Akori shouted. "Show yourself!"

123

Smoke rushed into the room, swirling into a tornado-like column. Two red eyes glared out of it, staring at Akori with unspeakable hate. A dark body formed, the muscular physique of a giant with the head of a wild beast. Set, Lord of Storms, the God of Evil.

"You are too late, little Pharaoh," Set said. "Say a funeral prayer for your beloved God. There is nothing you can do to save him."

"I'll strike you down," Akori warned. "Then we'll see!"

"Try then, whelp! Let's see how well you fare against the Lord of Storms!"

Akori held his *khopesh* up, ready to charge. "Ebe! Attack!"

Ebe yowled, arched her back – and nothing happened.

"Ebe?"

She looked up at Akori, her little feline face totally helpless.

Akori felt as if the ground was about to swallow him up. Ebe was unable to change into Goddess form! Carrying them from the market, fighting the masked mummies, battling Ammit…she must have used up too much of her power already.

Set threw back his head and laughed in cruel delight. "So, it seems you will be facing me *alone*, boy!"

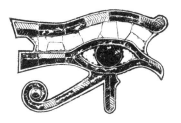

CHAPTER TEN

"You may wear the Pharaoh Stones under that cloak of yours," Set said, "but even their power will not enable you to defeat me." He drew his two *khopesh* swords. "You will remain in the Underworld for—"

Akori did not wait for Set to finish his boasting before he attacked. Hurriedly, Set brought his swords up to form a cross and only just blocked Akori's opening blow, a powerful two-handed slash from above.

Akori recovered, aimed a feint at Set's face

and scythed his sword across Set's waist when the God went to parry. The sword gashed Set's muscular stomach, making him bellow in shock.

"I'm sorry," Akori mocked, "weren't you ready yet?"

Set angrily swung at Akori with one blade and the next, striking high and low. Akori couldn't block both blades at once. Instead he simply launched into a forward roll between the slashing swords, past Set's huge body, and tumbled back onto his feet. Then he spun around and delivered a quick blow to Set's exposed back.

"A bold move!" Set growled, moving to face him again. "Let's see how you handle *this*!"

Half a dozen of the iron chains hanging from the ceiling sprang into life, lunging at Akori like striking serpents. One of them caught him across the face before he could get out of the way. It left a deep, stinging cut.

Akori severed the chain with one blow. It fell to the ground in a rattling heap. The others hung close by, wavering in the air like tentacles. A few swift blows with the magical golden *khopesh* chopped them down as if they were reeds.

Set snapped his fingers, ending the spell. "Hmm, swift and strong. You've grown up, farm boy."

"The power of the Pharaoh Stones runs in my blood," Akori said. It was true, he knew – the magic of the Stones was part of him now.

"Then that blood must be spilled!" roared Set. He ran in close. His immense arms windmilled, bringing the blades down one after the other with brutal force.

Akori could only fall back before the power of his attack, dodging and blocking where he could. Every time he repelled one of Set's blows, a ringing shock went up his arm, numbing his fingers.

He quickly glanced over at Manu. The priest was tending to Osiris as Ebe kept watch. But Set was too busy battling Akori to spare him any attention. And that was just how Akori wanted it.

The whirling blades kept coming, pressing Akori back further and further. He had to counter-attack somehow, but there was no let-up in the assault. In desperation he began to back up the stairs, praying he wouldn't stumble.

Set grinned, showing yellow razor-sharp teeth.

Without warning, Akori jumped from the staircase and caught hold of one of the iron chains that dangled from the roof.

"Get back here!" Set yelled. He flung one of his swords.

131

Akori let go of the chain and fell to the floor, hard. The sword missed him, but a searing pain shot up through his leg. He tried to stand, but his ankle gave way under him.

Set laughed as he realized Akori had twisted his ankle. "No more running," he said. "I have you now."

"Not while I still draw breath!" Akori panted. "Fight me!"

Set strode up to Akori and rammed his sword at his chest in a killing stroke.

Akori turned the blow aside. He tried to hack at Set's weapon arm with a reaching thrust, but fresh agony poured up his leg when he put his weight upon it.

Set's next attack smashed the *khopesh* right out of his hand.

Akori quickly looked at Manu, who nodded at him as if to confirm something.

Then, as Set began to laugh in victory, Akori punched him hard in the stomach. He pummelled the God's rock-hard belly with his fists as if he were a sack of flour.

"Still…fighting?" Set gasped. With a rattling snort of disbelieving anger, he drew back his sword arm and thrust with the force of a thunderbolt.

The sword pierced Akori's golden armour, passing through his body and out of his back. It crunched into the masonry behind him, pinning him to the wall.

Akori didn't even feel any pain. He looked down at the enormous sword skewering him to the wall and smiled. Death in the presence of Osiris himself. What Egyptian could hope for a better end?

"What are you SMILING about?" Set bellowed. "I've killed you, you fool!"

"You've lost," Akori whispered.

He could feel his life ebbing away with every word. But still, Akori was triumphant. *I did it,* he thought to himself. *I saved my kingdom. Even if Set doesn't know it yet.*

Set strode forwards. "Lost? How have I lost? Osiris is almost destroyed, you are dying, and I have the Pharaoh Stones back!" He reached up and with both hands, tore Akori's cloak apart. "Once I pull them out of that armour—"

He stopped.

Akori was wearing the golden armour of Montu, but the Pharaoh Stones weren't there. Set was staring at five empty hollows.

"I don't understand!"

"You always were…stupid," Akori said hoarsely. "And that's why you've lost."

"You fought me WITHOUT the Pharaoh Stones?"

"Yes," Akori breathed.

"But…you fought with such power, such strength!"

"Their power runs in my blood. I told you. You didn't listen."

Set stepped back, clutching his head in confusion. "But if *you* haven't got the Stones, then who has?"

"The God who was meant to be their guardian all along!" said a rich, deep voice from the darkness. "The rightful ruler of the Underworld!"

Set spun around.

Osiris was free.

He stood, great and powerful, the mummy wrappings coiled at his feet, and Manu by his side. In the ornamental golden collar he wore, the five Pharaoh Stones were shining. The anger on Osiris's face was rare and terrible. Demons would have fled from it.

"Akori asked Manu to return the Stones to

me, to restore my powers," Osiris said. "He tricked you into believing he still had them."

"He fought you even though he knew he couldn't win!" Manu said, tears running down his face. "That's how brave he is."

"He's dead!" Set roared.

Osiris shook his head. "I am Lord of the Underworld, dark brother, and I have power over life and death!" He raised his *ankh*, the symbol of life. "Be whole, Akori!"

The *ankh* flared briefly with light. Set's sword fell clattering to the floor.

Akori stood up, feeling an incredible new strength in his limbs. He walked towards Set, slowly and deliberately. There was no wound on Akori's face now, nor in his chest. His ankle was healed. He stooped, picked up his *khopesh*, and kept advancing.

"I beat you!" Set shrieked. "I killed you! *Get away!*"

Akori did no more than gesture with his hand. Set doubled over, gasping as if he had been struck. Another gesture, and Set crashed to the ground. The impact shook the floor and rattled the iron chains.

As he lay gasping and groaning, Akori raised his sword in a two-handed grip.

"In the name of Horus the Avenger, I cast you out!" Akori cried.

Golden radiance poured out of the sword, the colour of Horus's holy fire. It moved like a living thing, arching across the room and twining around Set like a serpent, burning away his dark power.

Set let out a terrible howl, as his body began to shrivel and collapse. He became a shrunken, ghostly wraith, a transparent scrap that was barely recognizable as the terrifying God it had once been.

"Assessors of the Dead!" Osiris called.

"I summon you!"

Forty-two shadowy figures slowly appeared, materializing out of the darkness. They laid hands on the struggling ghost-form of Set. The howling he made was like the squealing of a tiny, trapped animal.

"Take him to the furthest, bleakest limits of my kingdom, where none shall ever find him," Osiris commanded. "Imprison him there for a thousand years. Maybe, in time, he shall learn not to challenge the champions of the Gods."

CHAPTER ELEVEN

Manu ran to Akori and gave him a brotherly hug. "I thought you were dead!"

"I think I was, just for a moment," Akori said. "But since Osiris healed me, I've never felt so healthy in my life." A shadow passed across his face. "My Lord," he said, turning to the great God of the Underworld. "How are my people of Egypt? Are they safe? Please tell me the army has not attacked yet."

"Oh no!" said Manu as Akori's words hit home. "We must get back. I wonder if Aken has recovered from the demon vultures' attack."

Osiris smiled. "No need to worry about that. Now that my strength is restored, I can heal Aken in an instant." He began to ascend the stairs. "First, however, I have some business to attend to. Would you join me in my Hall of Judgement? You too, dear lady Bast."

Ebe purred and ran to join him.

When they reached the Hall, Osiris frowned a little to see the smashed pillar and the scattered mummy remains. He raised his hand, spoke a word of power that thrummed in the air like a plucked string – and the hall was restored. It shone with the splendour of finely carved marble stone, lit with hundreds of lamps burning with clear light. Ammit bowed her head to see her rightful Lord approach.

"Hear me, all you legions of the dead!" Osiris proclaimed. "It is I, the true Ruler of the Underworld."

His booming voice sung out from the Hall to all the caverns of the Underworld, echoing across deserts and resounding from tombs, ringing from the sky above the market and thundering out from open tunnels.

Dead soldiers stood still, weapons in their hands. Dead commanders hesitated on the verge of their great attack. Every dead soul in the whole Underworld stopped to listen.

"The usurper, Set, has fallen," Osiris declared. "The spells he cast to force you to obey him are broken. To all of you, whatever your misdeeds in life, I say *rest*. Embrace the peace of the afterlife. By my power, I set you free!"

Free. The word was whispered by the lips of countless thousands of the dead.

One by one, they were gradually released from the hold Set once had upon them. They let their weapons fall, dropped their shields, released their scrolls of battle plans. Their bodies dissolved into mist or poured away in dust. Ancient bones, no longer animated, fell with a dry rattle and a sound like sighing.

With a welcome sense of peace, Akori could now be sure that Egypt was safe.

Osiris clapped his hands briskly. There was a sound of wings beating, and one of the vulture-women who had attacked Aken's barge came swooping into the room. Now she was no longer corrupted, her face was beautiful and calm.

"Servant of the Goddess Mut, I order you to carry Akori and Manu back to Egypt," Osiris said. "As for Bast, I would be grateful if she stayed by my side for now. There is much that needs putting right in my realm."

Turning to their feline companion, both Akori and Manu each gave Ebe a fond stroke. "I'll miss you," Akori whispered. "Thank you for everything."

"I'll never forget you," Manu murmured.

Ebe purred, twined around their ankles, then trotted off to join Osiris.

Akori and Manu climbed onto the back of the vulture. "Thank you, great Osiris," said Akori, bowing his head.

"Wait!" Osiris said. "Akori, before you depart, I need you to take a message for me."

"Yes?"

"When you next see my son, Horus, tell him he chose his champion well!"

Pride and happiness burst inside Akori like a thousand blazing suns, as the vulture woman roared and spread her wings. Akori and Manu clung together as the creature flew out of the hall, and over the stone walkway.

Akori's heart missed a beat as, instead of continuing along its length, they flew over the edge and out into nothingness. The black ocean churned far below them.

They soared high above the Great Abyss, flying in sweeping spirals that climbed up and up. The vulture woman flew faster and faster, rushing as if she meant to break right through into Egypt. Akori held tight and put his faith in Osiris.

A dim light appeared in the distance. It wasn't a torch, or a bonfire, or an oil lamp. It was sunlight, shining in through a cave mouth. Akori whooped in joy as they powered towards it, getting closer and closer.

Bursting out into that glorious, light-filled sky was like diving into the sun itself. Akori laughed, feeling its warmth on his skin. Beneath, the familiar fields of Egypt spread out as if in welcome, and the Nile gleamed

up at him like the smile of a long-lost friend. There in the distance, looking no bigger than a toy, was the palace.

"Come on, Manu!" he shouted. "Let's go home."

Never had Egypt seen a celebration to match the Pharaoh Akori's homecoming. The tables overflowed with roast meat, luscious fruits, bread and barley beer. From one end of the kingdom to the other, the people rejoiced. The dead were back in the Underworld where they belonged, and their families could once again burn incense and leave offerings in their memory.

Akori stood at the head of his own grand table, with the God Horus on his left side and his High Priest Manu on his right. The old High Priest, though his nerves had suffered terribly during the troubles, was still able to join in with the feasting from the comfort of a cushioned bench.

"May the Gods bless Egypt, and all her people," Akori prayed. "May we live out our lives in peace and prosperity, and live for ever with Osiris in the world to come!"

"Well spoken, Akori," said Horus. "You have repaid my trust in you a thousand times over. My father was right. I chose my champion well."

"Is it over, then?" Manu asked. "Have we defeated evil?"

"Set will never cause Egypt such troubles again," Horus said. "But Akori's work – and yours – is far from over. Evil can take root in the hearts of ordinary men, too, from petty criminals to mighty tyrants. Egypt will need her mightiest Pharaoh and her wisest High Priest in the coming years."

Akori nodded. His people were laughing

and feasting as if nothing could ever go wrong again. But he knew, deep in his heart, that his great quest would never truly be over, because his people would always need his leadership. Being Pharaoh was not about having power and wealth, as Oba had always thought. It was about putting your people's needs above your own, for as long as you lived.

"Are you troubled, Akori?" Horus asked later on. "You are not eating."

"No," Akori answered honestly. "I was just thinking about all the work that's left to do."

"One last piece of advice, then, before I leave you." Horus smiled. "Celebrate! Today, you are victorious. Let your people *see* your joy. Life is short, and these moments do not come often!"

"Will we ever meet again?" Akori asked.

"One day, I shall welcome you into the

company of the Gods," Horus promised. "But that day is still a long way off. Feast and drink, my champion. You have earned it."

And with that, he became ghostly and translucent, then disappeared leaving an empty chair.

Akori smiled. Horus was right. Today *was* the time for feasting and celebration. He looked around him at all the people gathered in his palace, smiling and laughing, and felt a burst of pure happiness. He turned to see Manu talking with the old High Priest. Akori took a sip of his barley beer and went to join his friends.

COLLECT EVERY UNDERWORLD QUEST!

WICKED DEMON-BOY OBA IS RAISING AN ARMY OF THE DEAD TO ATTACK EGYPT.

ONLY ONE BOY CAN STOP HIM...

FIGHT OF THE FALCON GOD

Young Pharaoh Akori must
venture into the dark and deadly
Underworld to battle the fearsome
Falcon God. But will he
make it out alive?

ISBN 9781409562009

RISE OF THE HORNED WARRIOR

Akori must journey deep into the
Underworld to the labyrinth of
bones and fight the lightning-fast
Lord of Thunder. But can he match
the God's awesome speed?

ISBN 9781409562023

SCREAM *OF THE* BABOON KING

With dark magic invading the land, Akori must seek out Oba's Underworld palace and find the terrifying creature stalking his nightmares – the bloodthirsty Baboon God!

ISBN 9781409562047

CLASH *OF THE* DARK SERPENT

The Sun God has been captured by the gigantic serpent of the Underworld. Now Akori must defeat the beast, or else darkness will seize Egypt for eternity.

ISBN 9781409562061

DESCENT *OF THE* SOUL DESTROYER

Akori faces the ultimate challenge as he prepares to battle Ammit, the monstrous Soul Devourer. Can he succeed before Oba's army of the dead destroys Egypt for ever?

ISBN 9781409562085

FREE GAME CARDS IN EVERY BOOK!

CATCH UP WITH ALL OF AKORI'S QUESTS!

EVIL PHARAOH OBA HAS IMPRISONED THE GODS WHO PROTECT EGYPT, AND NOW BLOODTHIRSTY MONSTERS ROAM THE LAND.
ONLY ONE BOY CAN STOP THEM...

ATTACK OF THE SCORPION RIDERS

For his first quest, Akori must risk his life, fighting giant scorpions and a deadly Snake Goddess. But will his terrifying battle end in victory?

ISBN 97814095621051

CURSE OF THE DEMON DOG

The dead are stalking the living and Akori must send them back to their graves. But dog-headed Am-Heh the Hunter has sworn to destroy Akori...and no one has ever escaped his fearsome jaws.

ISBN 97814095621068

BATTLE OF THE CROCODILE KING

Akori must brave the crocodile-infested waters of the Nile to battle two evil gods – the terrifying Crocodile King, and his gruesome wife, the Frog Goddess – both hungry for his blood...

ISBN 97814095621075

LAIR OF THE WINGED MONSTER

Vicious vultures and deadly beasts lie in wait for Akori as he searches the desert for the Hidden Fortress of Fire – and the Goddess imprisoned there. Will he survive or will this quest be his last...?

ISBN 9781409521082

SHADOW OF THE STORM LORD

The battle to end all battles has begun. Akori must fight Set, the dark Lord of Storms himself, and beat Oba, the evil Pharaoh, to claim his rightful throne. But can Egypt's young hero finally win the crown?

ISBN 97814095621099

FREE GAME CARDS IN EVERY BOOK!

COLLECT THE CARDS AND PLAY THE GAMES!

BONUS BANDITS

The aim of the game is to boost your stat to become the ultimate bonus bandit!

Players: 2-4
Number of cards: at least 2 per player
Dice: 1

- Shuffle the pack and deal the cards face down to all players. Roll a dice to see who starts.
- *Player One*: pick a category for that round.
- *All Players:* turn your topmost card face up on the table.
- *Player One:* using the Under Attack! rules, roll the dice. If you roll an even number, add 400 bonus points to your stat. If you roll odd, you do not win any bonus points.
- *All Players*: take it in turns to roll the dice to boost your stat. The player with the lowest total score in the round puts their card out of play, while everyone else places their topmost cards to the back of their packs.
- *Player Two:* pick the next category and roll first. Play continues around the table.
- *LOSE*: players are eliminated when none of their cards are in play.
- *WIN*: when only one player has any cards remaining, they are the winner!

TURN THE PAGE TO DISCOVER EXCITING NEW GAMEPLAY OPTIONS WITH THE PHARAOH STONE CARDS...

EACH BOOK IN QUEST OF THE GODS
INTO THE UNDERWORLD
COMES WITH AN EXCLUSIVE PHARAOH STONE CARD

- Each Pharaoh Stone card is worth a number of bonus points. The further in the series you get, the more powerful the Pharaoh Stone card in the book, and the more bonus points available:

    Book 6: Stone of Courage = 50 points
    Book 7: Stone of Speed = 150 points
    Book 8: Stone of Strength = 250 points
    Book 9: Stone of Intelligence = 350 points
    Book 10: Stone of Honour = 450 points

USE THE POWERS OF THESE CARDS FOR EXTRA GAMEPLAY IN

SUPER BONUS BANDITS

◆ The rules are exactly the same as *BONUS BANDITS*, except that players should also have an equal stash of Pharaoh Stone cards each.

◆ After playing the Under Attack! rules, the losing player may use their Pharaoh Stone card to win the battle.

◆ The losing player rolls the dice. If they roll an even number, they add the Pharaoh Stone Bonus to their stat score. If their total score is higher than their opponents', they win the battle.

◆ If they roll an odd number, they lose the round and must forfeit their Pharaoh Stone card to the winner, who may now use it once more during the game. Each Pharaoh Stone card may only be used once by each player during the game.

THIS IS JUST ONE WAY YOU CAN USE THE PHARAOH STONE CARDS TO ENHANCE YOUR GAMEPLAY. TURN OVER FOR MORE BATTLE-BOOSTING RULES...

PHARAOH STONE CARD RULES

Use your Pharaoh Stone cards for extra gameplay with these crazy wild card rules. Just make sure all players agree which rules you are using before you start.

- An equal number of Pharaoh Stone cards are dealt to each player and kept separately from their main hand.

- Players may look at their Pharaoh Stone cards.

NB: A Pharaoh Stone card can only be used once per player, per game!

GETTING EVEN

- If a player is losing, they can try to roll the dice to boost their score by the amount of points on their Pharaoh Stone card.

- If the player rolls an even number, the number of bonus points on the card is added to their score. If the player rolls an odd number, they do not gain any bonus points and their Pharaoh Stone card is out of play.

ON A ROLL

◆ Rules are the same as *GETTING EVEN*, but if you roll an even number you automatically win the round, regardless of your score.

USE IT OR LOSE IT

◆ The rules are exactly the same as *GETTING EVEN*, but if you roll an odd number, you must forfeit your card to the winning player.

BONUS BUDDY

◆ The losing player may use their Pharaoh Stone card and add the bonus points to their current score without rolling the dice.

AUTOMATIC WIN

◆ The losing player may use their Pharaoh Stone card to automatically win the battle, regardless of their score and without rolling the dice.

Check out *SUPER STAT ATTACK* and *SUPER BONUS BANDITS* for gameplay options, or try *FIVE-CARD TRICK* for the ultimate Pharaoh Stone game.

FOR MORE FANTASTIC GAMES, GO TO WWW.QUESTOFTHEGODS.CO.UK

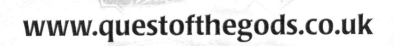